Gunilla Wolde

This Is Betsy

Random House New York

First American Edition, 1975

All rights reserved under International and Pan-American Copyright Conventions. Published in the United States by Random House, Inc., New York. Illustrations and original text first published in Sweden as *Emma tvärtemot* by Almqvist & Wiksell Förlag AB, Stockholm. Copyright © 1974 by Gunilla Wolde and Almqvist & Wiksell Förlag AB.   ISBN: 0-394-83161-6 (trade ed.)   ISBN: 0-394-93161-0 (library ed.) Library of Congress Catalog Card Number: 75-7566

Printed in Great Britain

This is Betsy
with a big smile.

But sometimes . . .
this is Betsy.

Usually when Betsy gets dressed
she puts her jeans on her legs.
That is the right way to wear them.

Sometimes . . . Betsy feels like
putting them on her head.
They look so much funnier that way.

Betsy knows the right way to put on
her sweater. She pushes her arms
into the sleeves.

Sometimes she puts it on the wrong way.
She thinks it looks funny. But of course
she has a little trouble walking.

On most days Betsy brushes her hair
until it is smooth and shiny.

But on other days she likes to make
her hair as messy as she can.

Betsy loves to drink cocoa.
She sips it from her own red mug.

But sometimes . . . when she feels like it
. . . she pours it into a saucer
and eats it with a spoon.

Betsy likes to build tall towers
with her blocks.

But sometimes the blocks fall down.
Then she is very angry.

Betsy loves her baby brother
and she usually shares her teddy
bear with him.

Then suddenly she feels
like snatching it away.
That makes her baby
brother scream.

When Betsy takes a bath,
she washes herself until she is
clean all over. It feels good.

But the very next day she plays with mud until she is dirty all over. That feels good, too.

Betsy can hear very clearly
when Daddy calls, "Time for bed."

But sometimes she hides under
a blanket and makes believe
she can't hear him.

When Betsy is feeling sleepy,
she puts on her pajamas and
gets into bed.

Sometimes she keeps asking for things. "I want a drink of water," or "Tell me a story," or "Can I have another drink?"

But after a while Betsy gets tired.
She snuggles into her bed and shuts her eyes.
This is Betsy fast asleep.